This

Angelina

book belongs to

· · · · · · · · · · · · · · · · · · ·

PUFFIN BOOKS

Published by the Penguin Group:
London, New York, Australia, Canada, India, Ireland, New Zealand and South Africa
Penguin Books Ltd, Registered Offices: 80 Strand, London WC2R 0RL, England

puffinbooks.com

Angelina's Christmas first published by Aurum Press Ltd 1985; published in Puffin Books 2002
Angelina Ice Skates first published by ABC Ltd 1993; published in Puffin Books 2001
This collection first published 2012
001 – 10 9 8 7 6 5 4 3 2 1

Angelina's Christmas Stories

Stories by *Katharine Holabird* Illustrations by *Helen Craig*

PUFFIN

To my grandmother, Dorothy Holabird   KH

To my grandsons, Nat and Will, with love   HC

Angelina's Christmas

Christmas was coming, and everyone at Angelina's school was working hard to prepare for the Christmas show. Angelina and the other children stayed after their lessons to rehearse and help decorate the hall.

When Angelina left school it was already dark outside. Large snowflakes were falling and Angelina was so excited that she danced along the pavement.

The cottages in the village looked warm and welcoming, with holly wreaths on the doors and Christmas lights shining in all the windows; but the very last cottage was cold and dark. Angelina peeped in the window and saw an old gentleman huddled by a tiny fire.

Angelina ran the rest of the way home and found her mother and little cousin Henry in the kitchen. She asked her mother about the man who lived all alone in the cottage.

"Oh, that's Mr Bell," her mother replied. "He used to be the village postman, but he's too old to work now."

Angelina decided that she wanted to make a Christmas surprise for Mr Bell, so Mrs Mouseling gave her some dough to make biscuits shaped like stars, bells, and trees.

Henry had a piece of dough too, and he made a nice big Father Christmas biscuit. "Look!" he said proudly. "I'm going to see Father Christmas tonight and give him this biscuit *myself*!"

"Father Christmas only comes very late at night after everyone has gone to bed," Angelina explained. "Why don't you leave your special biscuit out on a plate for him?"

Henry started to cry. "No!" he shouted. "I want to see Father Christmas!"

"Don't be such a crybaby, Henry," Angelina scolded, but Henry wouldn't stop crying.

The next afternoon Angelina and her mother
packed a basket with the biscuits, mince pies,
and fruit for Mr Bell. "Don't you want to help
Angelina take the presents to Mr Bell?" asked
Mrs Mouseling, but Henry only shook his head.

Then Angelina and her father went out to find a
Christmas tree for Mr Bell. Henry followed Angelina
and Mr Mouseling all the way to Mr Bell's cottage,
but he still wouldn't speak to them.

The old postman was amazed and delighted to see his visitors. He invited Angelina and her father inside, and then he noticed Henry standing alone in the snow. "Come in, my friend!" said Mr Bell with a smile, and he picked Henry up and brought him in near the fire.

Mr Bell's eyes were bright and twinkling. "Wait here a moment," he said, and disappeared up the stairs. Then he came down looking …

… just like FATHER CHRISTMAS!

"This is the red costume I wore once when Father Christmas needed someone to take his place at the village Christmas party," said Mr Bell with a chuckle, and he sat down with Henry on his knee. While Mr Mouseling made tea and Angelina decorated the tree, Henry listened to Mr Bell's stories.

"I used to go out on my bicycle, no matter what the weather was like, to deliver presents to all the children in the countryside. One year there was a terrible snowstorm and all the roads were covered with snow. I had to deliver the toys on a sledge, and if I hadn't glimpsed the village lights blinking in the distance, I would have been lost out in the storm." Henry listened with wide eyes.

When it was time to go, Henry reached into his pocket. "I made this," he said, "and I'd like to give it to you." Out of his pocket he took his big Father Christmas biscuit and gave it to Mr Bell.

"This is the best Christmas surprise I've had for many years," said Mr Bell, thanking Henry and Angelina for their presents. Angelina said she wished Mr Bell would come to her school show in his Father Christmas costume.

"That would be a pleasure," he said, smiling.

Mr Bell kept his promise: he came to the Christmas
show in his red costume and watched Angelina and

her friends dressed as sugar plum fairies
dancing the Nutcracker Suite.

Later all the children gathered round Mr Bell, and
Henry felt proud as Mr Bell handed out the Christmas
presents and entertained everyone with stories about
his adventures as a postman.

Mr Bell was never lonely at Christmas again, because every year he was invited to come to Angelina's school show dressed as Father Christmas.

Angelina
Ice Skates

Angelina absolutely loved snowy winter days when she could ice skate with her friends on Miller's Pond. The ice sparkled like glass and they raced across it in pairs, practising spins and twirls and figure-eights.

Everyone in the village was getting ready for New Year's Eve, and Angelina was preparing a special ice skating show. Her little cousin Henry wanted to be in the show, too, even though he often tumbled off the ice and fell into the snowbanks.

"We'll need someone to be the Snow King," said Angelina's friend Flora, pirouetting across the ice as the Snow Princess.

"I'll be the King!" shouted Henry, but then he tripped and slid into Alice, who was going to be the Snow Fairy.

"You'd be a better snow shovel!" said Alice crossly as she dusted off her skates.

"Don't worry, Henry," said Angelina. "Hold on to me and let's practise skating together."

They linked their tails and tried to skate in a circle, but it wasn't easy on the slippery ice. Just then Spike and Sammy, two big boys from school, raced by playing hockey and almost knocked them all over.

"HEY!" shouted Felicity, but the boys were already gone, laughing and yelling across the ice.

"Never mind," said Angelina, helping Felicity get her balance. "Let me show you how to skate backwards."

But, before long, Spike and Sammy tore past again, spraying snow in all directions. When they zipped through Angelina's rehearsal a third time, she got angry.

"Please stop interrupting us!" she scolded.

But the boys just laughed, grabbed Angelina's scarf, and tweaked Flora's whiskers.

"Little ballerinas can't catch us!" they shouted as they zoomed away.

Angelina and her friends chased Spike and Sammy all across the ice, and then Angelina made a huge snowball and hurled it at the boys.

"Great! A snowball fight!" Spike yelled, throwing one back at Angelina. Then everybody started throwing snowballs everywhere, and soon Miller's Pond was a blizzard of flying snow and shouting skaters.

They had so much fun, they stayed until Flora got ice down her neck and Alice's toes began to freeze. Then they trudged back to Angelina's house, feeling tired and frozen.

"What's wrong?" asked Angelina's mother.

"Our New Year's Eve Ice Dance is a mess," said Angelina sadly. "We haven't got costumes or scenery and Spike and Sammy keep bothering us."

"I can help you with costumes," said Mrs Mouseling. "And maybe the boys are teasing you because they want you to pay attention to them."

Angelina was surprised. "That gives me an idea."

The next day Angelina put on her skates and whizzed past Spike and Sammy, snatched their caps, and raced off laughing with the boys just behind her. They were very fast, but Angelina could do all sorts of tricky twists and spins and, just as Spike and Sammy thought they would grab her, she spun out of reach and they smashed into each other, collapsing on the ice.

Spike gazed at Angelina in admiration.
"You ballerinas are fast!"

"Would you like to be in our show?"
asked Angelina, tossing back their caps.

Spike and Sammy leaped up. "Yes!"
they shouted, skating in circles around her.

Sammy loved doing funny tricks and Spike, who could skate backwards, was proud to be the Snow King. Best of all, they helped Henry build a huge snow fort. "It will make a nice Snow Palace for our show," said Henry enthusiastically.

"What a great idea!" admired Angelina.

On New Year's Eve, the whole village dressed up and came to celebrate. Miller's Pond looked magical as the

performers skated on to the ice in Mrs Mouseling's costumes,
and Henry's snow fort gleamed in the moonlight.

When Angelina danced into the spotlight that night, she felt just like a real snow queen. Spike and Sammy did exciting leaps and jumps together and Henry was thrilled to be the King's attendant, while Felicity, Flora, and Alice seemed to fly across the ice like delicate snowflakes.

At the end of the performance, as the magic hour
of midnight approached and fireworks sparkled in
the sky, Angelina and her friends wished everyone
joy and peace, and they all sang and danced
together to welcome in the New Year.